XXX COCK TALES

EXPLICIT DIRTY EROTICA SHORT STORIES

DAKOTA DEECE,TRINITY STYLLER,
MACKENZIE HARNDEN, FARRAH SEAGER,
KENNA DIVENS

plicit Press

CHAPTER 1

BREAKING THE FALL

THE REST of the group disappears down the path, through the thick trees. Luke is on the ground, a thick sleeping bag between him and the earth. Around his ankle his shoelaces are tied tight, the sprain so severe it could be broken. His nurse, another hiker, Gillian, is twenty-three and *hot*!

The somewhat older Luke dares not hope that this tight-assed hiking enthusiast might be one of those pretty young things with an attraction to mature, experienced *daddy* types. And with his ankle out of commission, he's probably looking a little less attractive than he normally would.

Sweat rolls down her thighs, Luke unable to tear his eyes from the rolling beads dripping from the vicinity of her cunt. Gillian stands almost above him now, blocking the sun from his eyes while soaking the rays up on her lightly freckled back. He holds one hand over his eyes just above his brow and runs the chilled bottled water over his neck with the other. The heat is working all around him as he soaks some of it up through the earth despite the sleeping bag.

Gillian watches his discomfort for a bit, trying to figure it out.

It takes almost twenty minutes for them to get off the path slightly, to the protection of the forest canopy. The sound of a waterfall they had passed minutes before Luke's accident cools them subliminally. The earth is cooler thanks to the shade of the tall pines. Gillian has her hands on Luke's thigh helping him to get comfortable. She's so close to him now that the smell of her shampoo is in his nose instantly. The sun on her skin also accentuates her natural feminine scent and Luke's cock is solid in seconds. The timing of the erection is impeccable, his dick moving directly into her hand as it moves over his thigh.

With a healthy impressive cock Luke isn't embarrassed. A look passes between them that makes any further conversation unnecessary. Gillian has her hands running over the massive hardness beneath the denim while they find each other's lips. Luke manages to get his belt and button undone, Gillian's hands on his dick making it so hard that he needs to get it out of the jeans. She helps get the pants just below his ass so that his butt cheeks are directly on the nylon sleeping bag. His back is somewhat perched up against a thick tree. His super-large cock almost breathes an audible sigh of relief once it is out in the open. With Gillian's fingers on the meat, the tool throbs.

Luke can't help thrusting his meat up into Gillian's mouth just as she wraps her lips around the massive head. He holds the base of his dick while she places both her hands on either side of him. Her ass is high up in the air giving Luke an incredible view. He wants her out of her shorts and he wants her out of them now. She moves her butt from side to side, teasing him with the visuals, knowing from the pulsating penis in her mouth that he wants to tap that. The agile Gillian lets Luke's cock deep into her mouth and lets the dick hold her up by pinning her up in her throat, and uses her hands to remove her shorts, and then her panties, slowly, seductively, wanting to keep him hard and entertained. The pain in his ankle is soon forgotten.

Reaching for her ass his hands get as far as the small of her back. She eases herself down onto most of his cock so that his fingers at least fall on some of her ass. It's clear what he wants, but Gillian isn't done sucking his cock yet. This is one of her favorite things to do and so she intends to take her time doing it. Luke gives up his ass pursuit and relaxes into the spectacle that is the magnificent blowjob he is getting. She moves from between his legs and is on her knees to the side of him so that their bodies form a right angle. He can now see her mouth moving up and down over his thick dick. There isn't a chance in hell that his cock is going anywhere but deep inside her cunt now, no matter what manner of the beast makes an appearance out of the thick.

Her lips are back on his for a minute. They kiss deeply, Gillian letting Luke know what he tastes like. There is no chance of a sixty-nine, the pair not wanting to aggravate his ankle unnecessarily by moving him around too much. The kiss is deeply satisfying, sending vibrations through both of them that make them wish they were in a hotel room somewhere. But this isn't an altogether unacceptable scenario, and Gillian stands up in front of Luke's face to show him just how acceptable it is. Finally Luke has a decent grip on her ass and he pulls her cunt into his mouth.

Her pussy tastes like jasmine and smells like fresh earth. His tongue goes immediately for the inside.

Gillian rests her hands on the tree holding up Luke's back and lets her cunt dance around in his mouth. He licks it hard, biting onto the clit every chance he gets. She can't help fucking into his mouth now as he sends her into a complete state. There is nothing more that she wants now than to be fucked by the massive cock barely inches away. She knows though that if anyone will be doing the fucking it's going to have to be her. Her cock-wielding beau is somewhat indisposed. She lets him eat away at her a little longer, throwing her eyes in the direction of his cock which is so solid now that it needs no help keeping itself up. It points straight at her cunt.

The impressive shaft brings Gillian moving down towards it. It's as if her pussy assumes a life of its own, moving to feed itself regardless of what the rest of her body wants. The rest of her comes to the party quickly enough though and Gillian places her hands on Luke's shoulders, using her strong calves to lower her onto the dick she can't even see. Luke knows that he now just needs to guide his dick into her, the rest totally her show, and so he does just that. He holds his cock still until its head is settled inside her fleshy cunt. Then Gillian drops deliciously slowly onto him, his thick meat filling her completely.

Their faces are on each other as Gillian gets down on to her knees. Luke takes her lips into his mouth and gives her mouth the same gentle attention that her pussy lips are giving his meat. He wants to adjust himself but can't since this will require him to dig his heels into the earth. So he just lets himself settle into his position and into the fact that today, it is he who is going to be fucked. Gillian wraps her arms around his neck and Luke settles his face somewhere near her breasts. He bites into them through her top.

With her knees on either side of him, and with them

planted firmly into the ground so that she has all the balance she needs, Gillian starts her riding of the dick she hadn't known she wanted until it jumped up at her. She gives his dick the most delicious squeeze with every muscle in her vagina and then moves her waist towards Luke. Then she lifts up and away from him, pulling his dick with her as she moves the cunt-vice still tight. Luke exhales as her pussy settles back down onto the cock again, taking it all into her vagina again before increasing the pressure of her squeeze and then giving a slow release.

Over and over Gillian delivers these incredible motions, pulling Luke's massive member in any direction her vagina goes. With the strength and athleticism of a gymnast, Gillian doesn't let Luke's cock slip once as she maintains her hold. He is so turned on by the power in her cunt that he no longer knows what to do with his hands, banging them into the dirt on either side of himself as she starts to ride him faster and faster. Keeping her cunt wrapped on his cock she settles onto it harder and harder. His dick is so deep inside her now that even if he had her on her back on a good day he probably wouldn't have gotten that far in. But with the ball in her court and his cock under her control, she lets him in farther than she normally would have given his massive tool.

She gets herself off her knees without moving herself off of Luke's dick. Her feet are flat on the floor a little behind Luke, her legs open a little wider. She has to hold herself up now using Luke's neck, but he keeps falling forward. This doesn't deter her from bouncing her cunt up and down on his tool, even when her arms slip from his neck and her hands settle on his knees. He can now see his cock moving around in the entrance to her vagina and he manages a few thrusts using just the muscles in his ass. She lets out excited screams at his efforts. Her waist moves from side to side while Luke fucks her up and down, his cock touching every part of her pussy.

Gillian's body starts to move in a series of waves that start at her shoulders and end at her cunt. Her neck is thrown back and her head hangs behind her. These massive ripples feed so much pleasure to his cock that Luke is the one letting out little yelps now. He knows that he is so close to cumming now, and he wants to tell her. But he doesn't want her to stop what she's doing, both he and his dick absolutely loving it. He reaches for her waist and tries to hold her in place but not. She increases the intensity of her upper-body waves and adds to it a twist. His cock will never forgive him for stopping her now. He can't stop her. He also can't keep himself from blowing much longer.

Her cunt settles completely onto him suddenly and stops. The squeeze now is tighter than it's ever been. She doesn't move. He wants her to move but she doesn't. He wants to scream, thrusting hard into her but her pussy keeps his dick largely immobile. Then she lifts herself to him so that again she wraps around his neck, their lips on each other again. Slowly she lifts her pussy off of him, freeing his cock. Then her mouth moves over the shaft again and swallows it almost completely. She mimics with her mouth the pressure she had created with her pussy. To further imitate her vagina she moves her mouth up and down his cock in the same direction that her cunt had done. It isn't too long before Luke is back to *so-close-to-blowing-Gillian-is-about-to-swallow-his-seed.*

Again he manages a few upwards thrusts. The back of her throat is as hot and tight as the depths of her cunt. Gillian's mouth dances over Luke's cock now and the entire shaft starts pulsating steadily inside her. She is so excited by the consistency of his erection that her fingers dig into her vagina now as she too gets closer and closer to blowing. She sucks him harder and harder but moves no faster now that the rhythm with which her fingers move in and out of her vagina. Maintaining this steady rhythm and pace Gillian is soon rewarded with a steady trickle of warm cream from the cock in her mouth. She manages to swallow and suck at the same time as Luke lets her have what must have been at least a few weeks of cum buildup. Her pussy flows rivers over her fingers as she too has a fantastic fucking orgasm in the forest.

CHAPTER 2

CHEYANNE FUCKS THE GREAT ARTIST

I DIDN'T SEE myself as a help. I'm twenty-seven years old; I have soft curly black hair. No facial hair. Some say I have a babyface, except for my dark-thick eyebrows. I am an artist. I painted the El Dorsista of Pallon, Ecuador. Her tall figure stood beside an ancient Mayan monument she helped find and excavate. She was not only pretty with her Indian features and long dark roll-curled hair, but also her face shined like an angel. She did so much for Ecuador. I fell in love with the Dorsista. I had to recreate her. This painting became my greatest triumph to date.

Several galleries wanted it, including the New York Gallery and Boston Gallery. I chose to have my retrospective in a private showing at the home of Cheyanne, a wealthy Native American who owned several casinos. Cheyanne looked white with her long rolled curl ponytails. One behind each ear. Her soft smile formed to near dimples at the ends. Her C cup breasts moved seductively under her off-the-shoulder formal purple dress and black sandal shoes. My name spread across the top of her spacious parlor read: Aondre Bristol, African American New Humanism Painter. New Humanist painters believe in positive permanent values, moderation, dignity, and a dualistic existence.

That is why when I finished talking to one of the several gorgeous white female visitors, I went to the bathroom. I was surprised. I had my six and three-quarter inch, banana dick out. I waited as long as I could, talking to as many people as possible, asking what they wanted to see painted. When thirty-year-old Cheyanne slipped into the bathroom quietly, I didn't notice. She embraced me as I pissed. She let her hands drop toward my thick patch of black curly pubic hair, as she kiss-bit my right ear. Startled I lost concentration, but Cheyanne said, "I can handle it from here," She grabbed my soft phallic flesh around the base. Her fingers had a way of touching my balls too as she guided my stream of piss into the bowl. "Men should not wait that long. It makes them too eager to fuck and cum inside a woman."

I didn't know what to do. My growing fuck tool knew before me. Slowly I went from butter-soft to sausage hard. Then I went from sausage hard to dried petrified wood. I wasn't fully extended but Cheyanne said she'd solve that. She squatted, moving lower down my back to my buttocks. That was where she stopped. Her hot breath felt good on my buttocks as her tongue snaked out and started giving me a rim job, something I never allowed. I'm a man and I don't let anyone play with my butt. Her hot fingers still held my cock meat trapped. The piddle became a trickle and the harder I grew the less I pissed until I stopped entirely. My dick meat fought and struggled with Cheyanne's moist hot hands. Her perfume smelled like "She's Lovely Tonight", a fragrance worn by a lot of teenage girls. Somehow her body heat made the scent heavier and more mature.

As she licked my butthole, my penis size increased. She stopped and lowered her tongue again and slurped one of my tight balls. She rescued it from being smashed on my groin. Her tongue pulled my wrinkled sacs further into her wet warm mouth. At least she prevented my sperm from erupting out of the tube of my fuck pole. I almost blasted off. She hummed around my plums. Her hands stroked my cock up and down. Finally, she tested the waters, my slippery precum on the tip of my dick. "You are ready now, fully extended."

"And what about you, Cheyanne?" I said trying to turn my head and see her. "Flush the toilet. You must give no one the impression we fucked in here."

I did as she said. What else could I do? I wanted to fuck her as soon as I saw her. When she first came to my studio, a year ago.

Cheyanne talked about the trilogy she wanted. Now I understood. Balls, Penis, and Brain. She said, "A BPB trilogy delivered at the opening."

I never painted a trilogy, much less a BPB-styled one. Her raspy voice sounded then much like tonight—full of heat and desire. Full of things women are only now beginning to say outright, full honest straightforward expressions of their physical desires. Too long, we men have had our way. Now we must learn to become harp strings stroked, pushed, pulled, and plucked by sexually forward women.

Cheyanne's hand slid over my pussy fucker like oil. The skin on my dick slid easily back and forth making me fully aware of my blood-filled passions. If Cheyanne's hand felt this good, what about her puss?

She was still in her squatting position; her pussy scent playfully assaulted my nostrils. My nostrils told me that her love box dripped, wet. My dick-mind ran ahead of my brain-mind and I moaned. Cheyanne slowly turned my hips around to face her. My soft silky boner-hard dick tapped her white high left cheek. She moved back and lowered my dark tootsie roll into her melting mouth.

"Aggggggghhhh. Let's fuck Cheyanne. I need you!"

She sucked me into her mouth two times and stopped. She pulled back and examined her saliva oiled candy toy, she said, "A man must always ask!" She sighed heavily. She sat up on the full porcelain bathtub's rim. She didn't even bother to close her legs. Her purple formal dress hugged her twenty-three-inch waist.

I reached in and pulled out her conical tits pointing out to even tighter nipples. She dragged me down to my knees. My cock lined up with her hot snatch.

"I'm glad you are so tall. We fit perfectly." She pulled my face forward. I stopped manipulating her nipples and placed my brown hand on the side of her neck. We kissed.

Her cunt kissed and sucked my love rod into her deep cavern of lust. I went deeper and longer and her pink pussy ripples flowed over my dick until at last, she engulfed me.

Cheyanne said, "Don't move! What a perfect BPB trilogy. Thank you." Cheyanne proceeded to move and fuck me the way she desired. She wrapped my balls, penis, and brain into herself. In three minutes, I wanted to blow my spunk wad. "I'm in control of your trilogy. You want to last ten minutes."

Her confidence motivated my trio to comply. It took exactly ten minutes before her moaning and rapidly stuffing my bloated fuck rod in and out of her pussy made us both quake and cum. I grunted low and silent as I could.

She turned the bathtub water on high. She screamed. Her pussy quaked around my dick forcing more spunk blobs of man sauce into her cooter snatch.

"We are one now!" she said relaxing, her groin pressed against my groin. "Now you can really paint that trilogy.

CHAPTER 3

FLEXI-FUCK FIRST DATE

AS A FREELANCE JOURNALIST, I receive odd assignments. One on-the-spot assignment for my small newspaper covered the local women's rhythmic gymnasts. These girls are so flexible and athletic; they bend over backward and touch their heads to the floor while catching hoops, ribbons, and clubs with their toes, hands, and even the back of their knees. I stepped into the elevator of the convention center and this round face blonde goddess holding two clubs and a large hula-hoop smiled. I towered over her at 5' 8" to her 5' 2". Whatever she lost in height, she regained in sex appeal.

The girl's smile could melt steel. Her blonde hair was rolled tightly and was brushed back in a high bun. Her elegant posture and presence made having big boobs obsolete. Her buns under her pink warm-up suit left me speechless and horny to fuck her.

Whenever this happens to be around a pretty girl, I fall

back on Internet advice gleamed accidentally during my research on other topics. Rule #1 was when you don't know what to talk about; talk about what is obvious to everyone.

Undaunted, I said to her, "You probably know some great sex positions."

She smiled and hesitated. But she didn't blush. She ignored my opening statement entirely, "Hi my name is Jaylen. I'm a rhythmic gymnast." She adjusted her sporting tools and stuck out her right hand. I shook her hand and noticed the strong grip.

"Takes you sixty seconds to squeeze all the juice out of a mango, too."

Jaylen laughed, "I do know some great sex positions, but sometimes they squeeze all the fun out of sex."

I didn't understand at all, but our floor button light lit. She went to the competitor's end of the hotel room. I went to the Press end.

An hour later, I didn't expect to see her again. But there we were in the elevator. Jaylen wore a bright royal blue leotard decorated with gold stars and white stockings. Her blonde hair was in a high ponytail. This time her hands were free."

"Your creative flexibility can stifle sex?" I picked up where our conversation stopped. She said, "Visit my hotel room tonight."

· · ·

I took some great pictures of Jaylen. She won the hoop competition of rhythm gymnastics. The club's competition was tomorrow morning. I turned in my story and had the next two days off. I was free to watch the competition. More importantly, I was free to visit Jaylen.

When I reached her room, I knocked quietly on the door. Jaylen opened it wearing only her black bathrobe. She hushed me, "My roommate Elina is asleep."

We tiptoed into the living room and sat down by the couch. Jaylen pulled me close to her and she smelled like Pink perfume. I kissed her back. No. I held her slim body close to mine so tight her A-cup tits felt like C cup tits. She leaned on me and I fell back on the long black leather couch. "Let me show you something." She quietly said as she removed her robe.

I expected her to wear underwear. Jaylen didn't even wear panties! "What a pleasant surprise." She did a split on the floor, her right leg forward under her hips, her left leg behind her hips. Her clit popped out from her cute little cunt crease. She smiled big and wide. My dick jumped in my pants, anticipating an amazing deep blowjob. I pressed my hands to my crotch. I didn't want to scare Jaylen away.

Jaylen then stayed in the split. Quickly turning her torso she pushed her right leg horizontal with her left and faced away from me.

· · ·

My jaw dropped. I always wanted to bang a girl who could stretch out as wide and far as possible. "That's impossible, Jaylen," I replied.

"Not impossible. Different. Now fuck me!"

I wanted to fuck her, but when she said it, I didn't believe it! "I want to fuck you." I got down on my hands and knees. I kissed her neck and her back; she had the cutest little freckles on her back. The camera doesn't pick them up but in person. Wow!

I removed my pants.

Jaylen cautioned me, "Don't remove your shirt. In case, Elina wakes up." I found it impossible to fuck her.

She giggled. "If you find a way to fuck me, you can have me!"

Stirred on by the problems of necessity, I sat down behind her. I couldn't stretch my legs like her. I positioned myself beside her body. She kept peering back over her shoulder giving encouragement.

"There is a way!" she said.

Finally, I realized it. I sat down with my hip to Jaylen's hip. My legs were pointing in the same direction as her right leg. Then I picked her up and swung her around on my lap.

"You pay close attention to the competition." She giggled. "It took my ex-boyfriend in Russia two hours to figure out how to fuck me."

Once she was on my lap, I gently pushed her over facing my knees. She willingly fell over flat and her dull gray and inner pink pussy lips shaped like a heart honed in on my fuck stick. My cockhead dripped generous amounts of precum. I slid easily right up her fuck hole. She then rocked back a couple of times, gulping my man staff down her cranny cave. We were hitched!

Jaylen's pussy steamed and her girly goo coated my hardness in ten seconds. I got the amazing bird's eye view of her pussy swallowing my cock, while I stuffed her pussy sheath. She reached down and rubbed my thighs. I caressed her small boobs. Her boobs seemed especially soft and her distended nipples poked into my hot palms. I kissed her neck again because I loved the smell of her Pink perfume. Then Jaylen started fucking me harder. She turned around and her big blue eyes squinted, half-closed in ecstasy.

"I'm going to cum, Jaylen." "So am I," and she grinned.

The next thing I know, Jaylen pressed her hands on the carpet and lifted me completely off my thighs onto the balls of her feet and she jerked, twisted, and shamelessly humped my thick cock.

I couldn't hold back any longer. Watching her tight cunt circle give my bloated dick meat the blowjob of its life sent me right over the edge. I shot one squirt of man goo that hit her cervix. My cock muscles tensed again. I blasted another longer sperm wad inside her pussy canal. She quivered on my fuck pole for a minute then lowered her hands. She swiveled around, raising her right leg over my head, and locked both legs around my waist. That was for a warm-up now the flex fucking really begins.

. . .

When I left Jaylen's hotel room, my balls dragged in my pants. I didn't want sex for a week. But I always ask for a freelance assignment covering the Rhythmic Women's Gymnastic Championship whenever it is held in our town.

CHAPTER 4

FUCKING THE LADY OF
THE LAKE

WHEN I WAS CHATTING on Skype with my ex-girlfriend, she challenged me.

"Jack, you say you believe in the green lifestyle, but you've never gone camping, mountain climbing, or even gone to a park with a lake."

I didn't like losing an argument, so I told her, "I'm going to Kiwi Park in my home state, today. Right when I get off the phone."

Wendy knows where the park is because she used to live with me five years ago. She went on to better things, stripping up in New York City, and found a guy who likes doing all kinds of outdoor green stuff on her days off.

I hung up. "Half the day left to explore." I got in my Black Mazda and drove out to Kiwi Park. I checked out the map. I located the lake deep in the park and bought some groceries for lunch. Once I arrived at the small lake, I noticed how deserted it was. Very quiet. I laid out a picnic blanket of Green tea, vegetarian salad, cracker and cheese, and some ice cream sandwich bars left in the cooler. I wasn't there long before this nude woman showed up!

"They made this a nudist spot recently!" She walked past me in the buff. Her bright white skin reflected the sunlight. Her sexy strut bounced her long curly blonde hair off her shoulder blades. Her ass cheeks snared my eyes. People talk about Venus rising out of the sea. Well, this was Venus walking back into the sea.

The boner I got didn't go away. The smiling nudist slipped into the blue water inch by inch. Finally, she dipped her head under. After a second, she rose her head up from the water and flung her dark blonde hair back. An arch wave of water flew through the air and almost drowned my crackers.

She grinned. "I'm sorry about that. It's just I'm lonely and no one is around to notice me."

"Oh, I notice you!"

"If you noticed me," she cooed. "You'd join me."

I got to thinking about Wendy. Was I a green faker? "I'm coming in."

"The water's warm, really," she splashed some more water up on the dry land.

. . .

She saw my big dick freed from my black boxers. "You can't bring that monster in though." She laughed.

I laughed. I ran into the pond, her splashing me all the way.

When I entered the water, we got into a water-splashing fight. Even my hard-on managed to splash some water on her belly button jewelry.

I grabbed her and we sank into the warm water. Coming up for air, I said, "What's your name, Goddess of the lake?"

"Call me Guinevere!"

Guinevere's heavy tits had one-inch nipples. I lowered my head and Guinevere allowed me to take her nipples into my hot mouth, one after the other.

"I'm Jack."

She wrapped her legs around my waist and her love box fell right down on my sexkey. Guinevere reached down and positioned my hard desire next to her steamy hole.

I pushed and she locked her legs harder around my hips. We started fucking like two bunnies. The water made things especially easy. I didn't have to lift all of Guinevere's one-hundred and twenty-pound weight. Her height of 5'8 inches matched my own.

"I can't believe how suited we are for one another," I grunted as our joined fleshed rubbed against one another.

Guinevere kissed me and darted her pink tongue everywhere inside my mouth. Our lips locked and our tongues danced faster and faster. We finally came up for air and focused on fucking.

Her arms squeezed tightly around my neck. I palmed her butt and managed to even slip my thumb up her asshole. She really liked my thumb and moved in circles now instead of up and down. She ground her hips down on the base of my cock. My balls boiled as two months' worth of unused sperm begged for release.

Guinevere moaned in my ear after we stopped kissing again. She gasped. She confessed her search for the perfect Lancelot who wanted to achieve the Holy Grail. The hero is unafraid of the nature of man and earth and life itself. I confessed. I'd been a faker until I was challenged by my ex-girlfriend, Wendy.

We humped against one another harder. Our combined slippery lubes overpower the water's dryness. She loved my fucking motions. "You're good," she moaned. "Don't stop thrusting up deep inside me. Push harder against my cervix. I can take it!"

I held her hips, lifted her up, and pounded her down on

my firm hardness. Her spread butt cheeks slapped the water around us until huge circles flowed away from our naked bodies. I wanted to make her Prego. I don't know what came over me. Something in me wanted to settle down with children.

Guinevere opened her eyes. She opened her mouth. Every time I entered her, she opened her mouth. As I withdrew, she closed her mouth and hissed at me. Her wild blonde hair draped my shoulders and hers. She at one point entangled her right fist in my hair and demanded some sperm.

Somehow, time pressures and limits bring out my best performance. I started fucking Guinevere using a gusto known only to madmen deprived of sex for hundreds of years! I still couldn't believe I held this wet-dream hottie in my arms. All because I decided to go green! I liked the sounds she was making, mewing in my ear, hissing, and grunting. We both found a nice rhythm and I knew this was it!

I held her tighter, "I'm coming!"

"Sperm all my insides. Give me your man sauce!" "We're going to make a baby!"

"I can't wait to waddle around nine months from now!"

We hugged and pressed our flesh against one another. We didn't let go.

. . .

We came for what seemed like ten minutes. My fuck stick, so drenched in her feminine oils and my sperm, slipped right out.

We relaxed for a second and then came back on land. We lay on my picnic blanket. "I don't want you to leave me just because it's our first date!"

"I never leave a man after the first date," replied Guinevere.

Guinevere and I had a pretty baby girl one year later. We go camping as much as we can. We're going to be a green family unit in the future.

CHAPTER 5

MY EXPERIENCE WITH
MADAM DANIELLE (BDSM)

I WAS A RATHER shy guy in college. Most of the other students thought of me as a geek; a guy that could not get the attention of a female even if I was on fire and wearing a clown suit. I saw things differently as I was just a student that was devoted to my studies. I was not into the party scene and did not truly see the use of going out on a nightly basis and being wasted. I wanted to be something more than a well-hung jock who was only partying and fucking women because of my rather large endowment. I had some friends that kept telling me that I needed to lighten up and relax. I was not sure that I could do this. I was afraid that any deviation from my studies would lead to me not getting the passing grades that I needed to succeed in college. I had one friend, Brad, that suggested I try this place called the Power Trip for a place that would allow me to relax and let down some of the walls that I had built up. I was not certain about this but I also looked at things and saw that my grades were at a good level. I thought one Saturday night would not hurt anything. I decided to take him up on his offer and to head to the Power Trip and check it out.

· · ·

I arrived and was greeted almost as soon as I walked in the door by a woman who had a rather large set of tits. I was not really that keen on having sex, as I had never even felt a woman's breasts through her shirt. These tits were almost bare and I was a bit uncomfortable with the current situation. The woman tried to comfort me and get me to calm down. I had a hard time doing this. I was on edge and did not like things being out of my control.

A few minutes later a woman in a very tight and revealing leather outfit came out and greeted me. "I'm Mistress Danielle. I will be your master for the night. Anything I tell you is my command and you will obey. " I was not used to being out of control. I had always been in control and now this leather-clad power-hungry bitch was telling me what I was and was not going to do. I had a good mind to walk out and not take any more of this abuse from her. Part of me was curious about what was this experience going to involve. I went along and was led into what was called the playroom. There were a number of items on the wall as well as devices that I had never heard about let alone even seen.

"On your knees worm. You are going to learn to worship your master's feet and to learn the meaning of respect. I see you are a nerd type of student. I have seen them all. They come in and act like they have never been with a woman, then the minute I begin they all of a sudden have all of the experience that they spill out as to having in their life. You geeks, nerds, dweebs whatever you call them are all the same. You play women into thinking that you have never even seen a pussy and then all of the sudden you are giving the woman the time of their life and they cannot get enough of you. I bet you are just the same as all the others."

"No ma'am, I have never been with a woman. I am a virgin and have never even seen a woman naked before."

"You are saying that you have never seen a woman's breasts or smelled her snatch. We will see. I am going to test you and see if you are telling the truth. And another thing, do not speak unless I talk to you do you understand?" This question was greeted with a harsh slap across the face from Mistress Danielle.

I was ordered to strip and take every bit of my clothing off. Mistress Danielle took her clothes off as well and kept the whip in her hand. With me still on my knees, she came over to me grabbed the back of my head and shoved it into her cunt. I was being forced to eat her snatch out or suffocate in the process. I did what came naturally and began to work the woman's slit over with my tongue. I had heard my room-mate and others talk about what they called "eating a woman out' but had not actually seen this done and certainly never even came close to doing it. The more I licked the less intense her grip on my head was. I actually was getting used to what I was doing when I heard the woman I was with beginning to moan. I had heard my roommate's girlfriend enough times that I knew that I was doing something right. I kept doing what I was and soon the woman that was dominating me became even wetter. I was picked up and led over to the table that was against one of the walls. I was placed on the table and strapped into place. I was not able to get up and had to stay in place. Mistress Danielle came over and mounted me. Before this, she placed a rubber on me and then mounted me up.

Mistress Danielle got into the reverse cowgirl position and began to glide up and down in a hurried motion. I was torn, as I was not fond of the fact that I was being forced to have sex with a woman and yet, I was thrilled to be having sex with a woman for the first time. Mistress Danielle went up and down faster in a hurried manner. I was almost unable to control myself. I had never felt this type of feeling before and I had to admit that it was awesome. I had only masturbated a couple of times in the past and even that was rare. I was really getting into the actions that were going on and had to admit that I was glad that I was being forced to have sex with this awesome of a woman in front of me. I finally finished up and shot my load off into the rubber. A little of the cum leaked out and went into her cunt. Mistress Danielle whipped me with the whip and told me how bad I was. When I was done, she stepped out of character and congratulated me on having my first sexual experience. I found out that my friend had set the whole thing up and was determined for me to get my wings in the sexual experience club.

ABOUT THE AUTHOR

Dakota Deece is an emerging erotica author of many erotica kinks and sub-genres. Be sure to check out other books and leave a review if this story got you hot!

Visit my blog at Dakota Deece's Blog

Join my newsletter for the exclusive Dakota Deece's Newsletter

Sign up for Free Stories from Xplicit Press Authors

Xplicit Press Author Updates

Like Xplicit Press on Facebook

Follow Xplicit Press on Twitter

Readers: I want to expand a few of the stories to see where the characters can be explored further. If there are any of the stories that you would like to read more about again, I'd love to hear from you!

Keep In Touch
Dakota Deece
info@dakotadeece.com